The artist gratefully acknowledges the permission granted by Maurice Sendak for the use of characters from *Where the Wild Things Are*, ©1963 by Maurice Sendak.

Printed in Great Britain. First U.S. Edition 1987.

8   9   10   11   12

Library of Congress Cataloging in Publication Data
Willis, Jeanne.   The monster bed.
Summary: A little monster is afraid to go to bed because he thinks humans will get him while he is asleep.
[1. Monsters—Fiction. 2. Bedtime—Fiction. 3. Fear—Fiction. 4. Stories in rhyme] I. Varley, Susan, ill. II. Title.   PZ8.3.W6799Mo   1987   [E]   86-10366
ISBN 0-688-06804-9
ISBN 0-688-06805-7 (lib. bdg.)

THE MONSTER BED

Jeanne Willis · Susan Varley

Lothrop, Lee & Shepard Books • New York

Never go down to the Withering Wood!
The creatures who live there are up to no good:
There are gnomes that are nasty and trolls that are hairy,
And even the pixies and fairies are scary.

For a monster, young Dennis was very polite.
He tried very hard not to bellow and bite.
But one night he bellowed, "I *won't* go to bed!
I'm frightened! I'm frightened!" the wee monster said.

His mother said, "Why? There's no reason for fright.
I'll give you your bear. I won't turn off the light."
"The humans will get me," cried Dennis. "They'll creep
Under my monster bed while I'm asleep."

"Oh, no, dear," his mother replied. "That can't be.
Humans are only in stories, you see.
Because they're not real, they won't trouble your rest.
Get into bed now, dear. Mama knows best."

But when she bent down to kiss Dennis, he chose
To fasten his fangs round her warty old nose.
He tied up his toes in a knot round her knees.
"Led go of be, Deddis, you're hurtig be, please!"
"Promise the humans won't get me tonight!"
"Yes, dear, of course," said his mother. "Sleep tight."

He took off his pillows and blankets, and said,
"From now on, I plan to sleep *under* my bed.
If I'm underneath and a human comes near,
It won't think to look for me, safe under here."

So there Dennis lay, staring up at the springs,
Thinking of birthdays and chocolate and things.

Now, a bad little boy had played hooky that day
And gone into the woods, where he'd soon lost his way.

Too cross and too tired to walk anymore,
He came to a cave and went in through the door.
There was a bed, and he needed some rest—
So he threw down his satchel and quickly undressed.

But somehow he didn't feel sleepy. He said,
"If my mother was here, she'd check under the bed
In case there's a monster (or goblin or elf)."
Since his mother was *not* there . . .

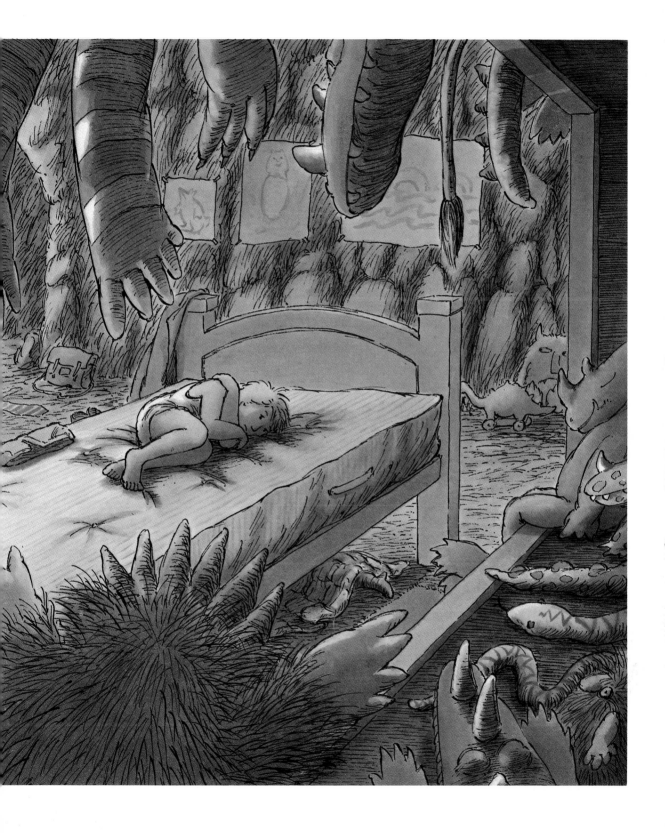

HE DID IT HIMSELF!

From now on, dear reader, you'd better behave.
Don't go to the woods, or to Dennis's cave,
Or you might meet his mother—just think how you'd feel
If she were to tell you that *you* are not real!

Other books by Susan Varley
Badger's Parting Gifts
The Fox and the Cat (written by Kevin Crossley-Holland)